I0624556

© 2014
by salem
All Rights Reserved

Published by
Metapulp, Inc.
New York

First Edition
A Paperback Imprint 2014

Library of Congress Cataloguing-in-Publication Data

salem, 1969-
Pearly Incognito / salem

p cm

ISBN 978-0-9894161-2-2

PEARLY INCOGNITO

BY SALEM

"The gem cannot be polished without friction,
nor man perfected without trials."
— *Chinese Proverb*

1: Pearly

Pearly considered the outline of his glass teeth with a curled red tongue. His face was round, his pallor opalescent and his ornamental canine teeth jutted like spear-fishing barbs. They were carved, tooled over time with designs reminiscently angling the seashore motifs of an ocean culture. In New York City he frequently was mistaken for some kind of modern primitive, a new wave dada-prosthesist or, from time to time, a light fixture of sorts. The latter was due to the rather common beaded metal pull chain dangling from the side of his head.

He had the chain installed to turn the light on inside his mother-of-pearl exoskull. Without it he could not see. Naturally the chain also turned the light off. There were some things Pearly, like any man, just did not want to see.

But Pearly, of course, was not a human man. He was male and mentally somewhat like one. He had human-like legs, a torso, arms and hands—even a neck. It was just his pearly, eyeless head, ornamental glass teeth and silvery skin that set him apart. That's all.

And his hooves.

Pearly donned a custom ski mask, pulled the chain and examined his reflection in a mirror.

There he was: a globe-like head, wrapped in the mask, topping a long linear frame. His humanesque body wore a gothic black suit. He really preferred his pink suit, but it was not anything he could wear in public without attracting even more attention than he already got.

He had come into being first as a shadowy, phantasmagoric projection cast out of a magic lantern. It was the Kirk's imagination, with its fervent apocalyptic fury, that had birthed him, or so he liked to imagine. Like the spiraling canine thrust from the forehead of the narwhal—a bizarre predicament of nature—he too had come to life. At least that was one biography he had created for himself. He could not recall his adolescence. He had no known relatives. The first memory he could pinpoint was of a fuzzy sentience. He had heard someone address him as Pearly. His next memory was snake-like. He heard his mouth hiss, felt his head strike and felt the pinpricks of his teeth puncturing skin.

The only person who ever knew him personally spoke his name but once, just before he died. Was murdered. Drank to death. By Pearly.

It was the 111th anniversary of the killing. Pearly turned a mother-of-pearl plastic amplification dial on his head. It was opposite the pull chain. The analog numerals one through ten were stenciled onto it. The same fellow who had installed the pull chain—a Chinatown analog robotics junkman—had installed the knob. It was harvested from an old AM radio and connected to an old audio memory chip lifted from a Pong game board. Pearly now turned it up. From audio memories he had collected over the years, he played the sounds of human beings crying. He bowed his head in somber memory and prayer, and in his imagination—which was the most powerful faculty he possessed—he cried with them.

His mouth opened. His glass teeth shone out from his black mouth—a fierce white light somehow escaping gravity—and he sobbed.

Oh, how I wish that I could have an eye, and that the eye could bleed but one tear!

2: Diamond Dada

Diamond Geet sat in the Diamond District of Manhattan and watched with envy through binoculars. His competitor across the street had struck it rich after he invented diamond body enhancement. It had started with war veterans and para-olympians wanting exotic limbs. Pop culture icons soon took up the trend. It was not uncommon to see someone famous strutting out of his store sporting a brand new diamond leg. Paparazzi were always stationed outside, hungry to capture images. The trend was named Diamond Dada, after the store.

His binoculars flashed with a curious light, and Geet could no longer see across the narrow street. He lowered the binoculars and saw a street lamp he had never noticed. Then it moved with incredible, inhuman speed, donned a bulbous ski mask and was quite suddenly standing right in front of him. The bells on the store door jangled as it shut.

Geet was about to scream, but the robber put his finger up to where his lips should be.

"I'm not here to rob you. I'll gladly pay you for your jewelry." Pearly showed him a roll of quantum bills. "I just don't want you to see me." His voice was even and clipped, as if he were a voice-over advertiser for a new soap.

Geet swallowed hard. His hands were shaking badly, and he could not find his own voice.

The man with the globe-shaped head stepped back. "I did not mean to frighten you. Unfortunately, I have this effect on everyone."

"What do you want?"

"I want you to make me a toothbrush."

3: Confessions

Pearly left his instructions then promptly made his way to a bank. There were several to choose from. He spied one that only had a few people milling around inside, and he slipped in, motoring himself with utmost speed and grace on his sprightly hoof-feet. He came to a stop in front of a teller.

The teller gasped, witnessing his ski mask. Pearly pushed a paper sack under the safety glass.

"Empty your drawer. Acetate. Thousands only." Pearly drew a gun out of his pocket and stealthily aimed it at her. She quickly complied.

He knew the routine. Her finger was on a buzzer. A dye-pack bill was being inserted between other bills; all of the standards. Pearly fled with his usual speed and had just enough time to ferret through the bills. His long, tapered and pale silver fingers nimbly rifled, finding the dye-pack bill—it was a bright red this time. He tossed it down a subway entrance before he rocketed out of Midtown.

A couple of minutes later he entered a kirk.

He waited in the rear on a wooden pew for his turn. He kept his overcoat collar high and a dark hood over his head. He kept his head bowed. His clothing was bespoke, tailored by himself. This suit's pattern was like an abstract painting rendered on various blacks, some of which shone or reflected light. It helped camouflage him.

When his time came he shuffled into the booth with normal human speed. Candlelight flashed in his suit's stitching before the darkness of the confessional chamber consumed him.

His mouth opened, revealing the many long, needling teeth that protruded from his black-red gums between the two nine-inch-long canines.

"Dear Father," he said. "I've come to confess my sins."

"Yes, my son. Speak."

"I killed a man 111 years ago."

On the opposite side of the dark wooden confessional booth, the priest's eyebrows hunkered. He'd been hearing this confession for as long as he had been a priest at this kirk.

"Anything else?"

"No, that's it."

"Very well, then. I suggest you perform 111 Hail Marys."

"Oh, come to think of it, I've killed some other people. And I recently robbed a bank."

"Son, you understand, I must believe everything you are telling me is the truth."

"It is the truth. I can't help myself. I just want forgiveness."

"All right. Perform 333 Hail Marys. And make a donation to the Kirk." The priest prayed, "Through the ministry of the Kirk, may God grant you pardon and peace. And I absolve you of your sins, in the name of the Father, and of the Son, and of the Holy Spirit. Amen."

Pearly humbly responded, "Amen."

Pearly stuffed a wad of quantum thousands into a donation jar on his way out. The rest he would need to spirit into Chinatown, to get the quantum encoding scrambled before the Q Bank landed on his trail.

Just then neon-pink lighting washed through a series of glass towers, animating an advertisement for a soap named Valentine's Day. The pink scintillated in his suit's reflective stitching. As he hastened toward Chinatown, zigzagging along the blocks, keeping pace with the advertisement as it jumped from building façade to façade, he blended in with the pink smear. His hooves clipped along the hard concrete sidewalk, the trotting sounds dampened by thick rubber boots fashioned from old tires. When the advertisement ended at Canal Street, bright neon-green crocodilian scales replaced it. This advertisement, he witnessed, declared no product. He paused on a busy corner and stared up at the phenomenon. The reflected light twirled through his suit.

Here, in Chinatown, he could stand still. There were monsters of all kinds on Canal and below it.

The crocodilian scales faded, replaced by darkness.

Another blackout, he thought as he slipped up a stairwell to Mock Duck's Money Laundering Services, Inc.

4: Q Bank

The Q Bank police gathered outside the Midtown kirk. It was an unwritten rule that stolen money—once it entered a holy place—could not be repossessed. The thief had been dumping money here for years, and there was nothing they could do about it.

Afterward it made its way to Chinatown with a speed they could not account for. Even the machine-gun-armed Postal Service could not transport anything this quickly. It was also an unwritten rule that once money made its way to Chinatown, there was no following it. The Millioni Mob ruled the boundaries of Chinatown. The mob had meaty control before the Central Library was burned down, but ever since the Great Fire they'd become ruthless. Chinatown had become one big black hole blighting the face of Manhattan.

"Migraine!" an officer shouted to the lead investigator, waving him to the kirk's stone steps. He pointed to the street, to a black gas-guzzler, a limousine.

"The priest's chauffeur. Switched from sunjuice to gas."

"Interesting." The lead investigator, John "Migraine" Megrim, entered his report by voice. Back at the Q Bank headquarters in Midtown he filed the new report in an ever-fattening manila folder. The computer files about the case filled a tetradrive, but he maintained a secret analog copy inside an antique metal file cabinet. Hammered into the face of a black plastic label by an old Dymo, protruding stretched white lettering labeled the case: DEAD END.

The case, or his job—or his life—had been giving him a massive headache for years. As his shift came to a close he made his way to a bar, one where Midtown Q Bank cops liked to meet up for a drink or two. He settled in next to a friend.

"Hey, Ruthie."

"What's up, 'Graine?"

"Another robbery today."

"The light bulb guy?"

"Apparently."

Ruthie waved the bartender over. "'Graine's first is on me."

Migraine slipped a small transparency out of a pocket and set it on the bar in front of his friend. She observed it as it illuminated with a high-res image of the robber from the bank.

"This is the best image we've got."

"Jesus. What's he wearing under the mask, a fish bowl?"

The transparent card went dark.

"Damn it!" Migraine tapped the card hard against the bar. "Fucking Oroboros."

Ruthie laughed and slid his drink close to his hand.

Migraine grunted. "You'd think Q Bank, the mother of all money corporations, could get me a virus-protected card." He slapped the card down and knocked back his shot of whisquila.

Ruthie stared at the card and tugged at his sleeve. "Look."

He glanced down. White lettering illuminated slowly with the phrase, *The Broker*.

5: The Toothbrush

Diamond Geet sat at his bench peering through his magnifying visor. It displayed the diamond granules embedded into thick paper. It was essentially sandpaper made of low-grade diamond dust. No customer had ever asked for him to make anything from industrial-quality diamond. At first when the strange man-thing had asked him to make a toothbrush, he'd swelled with pride and hope, imagining a diamond-encrusted handle.

But it was the bristles, the man had told him, that needed to be of diamonds.

Geet next examined the head of a high-end nylon toothbrush, an O-Brush. The nylon was extruded to nanometric diameters so fine the naked eye could not see them. Clustered together in the millions, they combined to form a plush head. Once vibrated with ultrasonic frequencies, they cleaned teeth in the same way surgical instruments were sterilized. The manufacturer of the O-Brush had branded its brushing sensation as orgasmic.

Geet muttered to himself, "How can this damn company make a sexy toothbrush out of freaking nylon. And I can barely make a diamond sexy!"

He flipped his visor up and stared through his storefront glass, to across the street. Geet had inherited the diamond business from his father. Growing up on Staten Island the last thing he had wanted to do was follow his father's path. His father forced him to work and learn the trade during his youth, but when it came time for higher education, Geet knew he was a Wall Street man. His thesis was on the formation of synthetic currency, and he had dreams of becoming a forerunner in the development of quantum currencies.

Just as he was a step, or more, behind Diamond Dada, he learned he was miles behind what had long been in development at the Federal Reserve. As time passed—and the best job he could find was as a low-level trader—he discovered the Feds only hired chess-gaming geniuses to assist with currency research and development. And Q Bank? It had come out of nowhere. One day it did not exist. The next there was one on every block.

Geet flipped the visor back down. On the outside of his visor, the magnifying glass mirrored his brown skin, his dark brown eyes and thick blackish eyebrows. His long black lashes flicked at the glass. In order to meet his client's deadline he would have to cancel a date. Of this he was actually glad. It was only a second date. The woman talked too much.

Whatever he lacked as a diamond designer he made up for in good looks and charm. He bent over the nylon bristles, enhanced his vision to microscopic and set about plucking each bristle from the O-Brush. It would be a long night embedding each strand with diamond dust.

6: Mock Duck

Mock Duck completed siphoning the value out of the stolen currency, and he replaced the acetate bills with non-traceable quantum currency. The bills would still each have a value of a thousand each, but after they were used they would bypass the Q Bank system and enter a twin system that Chinatown controlled. On the other side of Canal Street, whenever a vendor received a clone, they really had no way of telling the difference between the monetary systems. Only when they deposited to Q Bank did the original system acknowledge the rift.

But Q Bank was paramount, powerful and—it assured the Federal Reserve—infallible. Q Bank had come about to secure the socio-political-financial system and was a subsidiary of America, Inc. If they announced the system had been hacked, the economy could collapse into mayhem.

Mock Duck worked for the Millioni Mob. They brought him back to life after they discovered his DNA embedded in an old wool suit displayed in a museum. The adjustment to the new world had been difficult at first. He thought he had come to life in some kind of candy-colored nightmare. *Hell*, he thought, *I didn't even have a word for neon!*

They fitted him with special irises that dampened the neon, charring it into gray tones and the colors he remembered from his days as the Lord of Murder Alley. Through these irises he observed his customer, the man with the pearl head and the fangs. The man brought in money once a week. Single-handedly he was making Chinatown even richer than it already was. Marco Millioni himself had advised Mock Duck to treat the man with utmost respect.

"All done," he sang out. He slid the acetate bills into a cylindrical container, pushed the container into a tube and pressed a button. The tube sucked the container to the bare stainless-steel room that Pearly was waiting in alone. He had never laid eyes on Mock Duck.

And Mock Duck, having heard the grim stories about those who got too close to the man, though somewhat undead himself, was absolutely grateful for it.

7: Migraine

Migraine took an upway to his apartment. The train was one long flexible car that slithered along the uptracks to the buildings straddling the top of Old Manhattan. The pain in his head felt like a razor-edged clamp, and he was anxious to place his head onto his quantum-memory pillow. It was tuned to give him good dreams. The dreams helped soothe the pain.

The train docked at his building, an unremarkable black-glassed concatenation of cubes. His door scanned him as he stepped in front of it, then the lock popped and he entered. Smartlamps glowed to life. He kept them low. It helped ease the headaches.

A faucet automatically filled a glass with water. He picked it up, popped an aspirin and washed the pill into his throat. The glass made a clink against the granite counter as he set it down. He looked at it for a long moment. *Water*, he thought, *the only thing that's clear in my world.*

He had no memory of life before Q Bank. He removed his jacket. The emerald green quantum-thread-embroidered *Q* flashed under the dim light as he hung the coat on a chair. Something else flashed through the thin, bullet-proof carbon fabric. *My card.* He pulled the card out of a pocket. It was glowing bright white, so bright he could feel the heat. Then, in black lettering, the words appeared again: *The Broker.*

"Fucking Oroboros."

The letters transformed: "Not Ororboros."

"Right. Of course not."

The letters transformed again, into a copy of the black label on his analog file: DEAD END.

Migraine's eyes squinted. The reason he'd named his analog files with an analog label maker was to keep them away from the Oroboros virus. Only he knew about it.

"Who are you?"

The card reassembled the letters: "The Broker."

"I got that."

The letters reassembled again: "Mailman."

There was a knock at the door. Migraine muttered, "Fuck." He pulled his gun from his holster and entered the bulletproof chamber Q Bank had installed inside his home. Within it, a surveillance monitor revealed a bulky mailman clad in his standard gray uniform standing outside Migraine's front door. Over his shoulder was slung a machine gun. In one hand he held a small black envelope. Everyone knew mailmen only delivered bad news, and if you didn't let them deliver it, they would kill you. That was the urban legend Migraine recalled.

A mailman had never visited him, and the man's calm behavior disturbed Migraine more than the gun. Migraine spoke through the intercom. "What do you want?"

"You've got mail."

"I see."

"You don't have a mailbox. You'll have to open the door."

Migraine swallowed and waited a moment too long.

The mailman fired at the door's locking mechanism, destroying it. He pushed open the door and plodded inside on heavy black boots. "Where are you hiding?" He spotted the bulletproof chamber. A slit opened up on the front face, and a sign illuminated with the word, *MAIL*.

The mailman dropped the envelope into the slot. He lowered his chin to his shoulder and spoke into his old analog radio. "Delivered." He turned and methodically exited.

A long moment passed before Migraine felt the mailman would not return. He glanced down at the black envelope and realized the mailbox must be part of Q Bank failsafe protection. His name was typed in white ink on the face of the envelope. He bent down and retrieved it. He flipped it over, examining every edge, then reluctantly, he opened it. He withdrew a small black card that read: *To the roof. Now.*

Migraine hesitantly left the bulletproof chamber, slipped back into his coat and took the elevator to the roof. Curiously, he felt his headache being soothed away by the intrigue. Once at the roof he walked in a three-sixty, scanning the horizon of endless city. A small black helicopter landed, and its passenger door opened. A hand waved him in. He walked cautiously toward it, and once close he peered into its interior darkness. He saw a man wearing lightly tinted orange glasses.

"Are you The Broker?"

The man said, "I represent one. A crime broker. I have an offer for Q Bank. Please, come inside."

8: Hail Mary

The limousine chauffeuring Father Nuncio pulled up to the recycling center in Garbage Park. This area of Brooklyn earlier had been named for the legendary sunsets that in the past could be viewed from the park itself. Father Nuncio was not old enough to remember sunsets. But he was just young enough to know that the Kirk was run by the mob. He had been a young man when the self-proclaimed murderer first confessed to him. He was obligated never to inform the police, and as time passed the police became insignificant. When the rest of the United States, as they had been called, became New York City's dumping ground, garbage men came to dominate.

A man in a drab green uniform gestured to them, and the limousine slowly glided inside the gated center.

Father Nuncio stepped out onto the asphalt paving and was escorted by the uniformed man. The priest carried a small briefcase fabricated from quantum interference metals. Once inside the two made their way on a catwalk in between massive machines and conveyors sorting through trash. At an office door the uniformed man politely nodded, indicating the escort was complete. The door opened automatically and Father Nuncio entered the room.

A man with darkish skin and a trim, natty beard puffed on a cigar. His lips rose into a smile, revealing his white teeth. His eyes were made tiny behind nearsighted lenses. His nanoretina enhancement surgery had been botched on purpose so he could escape retina identification. Milky scars crisscrossed his corneas, and through this haze and the cigar smoke, he saw the outline of the priest. "Heard your patron saint stopped by."

"Yes." Father Nuncio set the case on the desk and took a seat.

"How much?"

"A hundred thousand."

"Payday! Thank god Jesus needs his garbage picked up, right?"

The priest slowly consented with a nod. The Garbage Gang had been holding the Kirk hostage for years, taking a hefty percentage of the Kirk's vast wealth in exchange for garbage removal and protection. "Q Bank officers were on the front steps again this evening."

The bespectacled man clicked a button on his desk. A tactile digital image unfolded in front of them, revealing a garbage-truck-meets-tank driving down Park Avenue past the Q Bank headquarters. He stubbed his cigar into an ashtray. "And we are on their front steps. Look, we don't rob their fucking bank! Fuck Q Bank!" Spittle shot from his lips. "Ha! We just rob you!"

Gloveless—his name was stitched in black over a pocket on his drab green uniform—had started out as a low-level sanitation worker. Known for his "gloves off" menacing approach to just about everything, he had quickly risen in the gang ranks. In order to prove himself superior to the last boss standing above him, he strangled the man with his bare hands on a live broadcast of Alpha TV. Gloveless was the alpha male of garbage, and Father Nuncio was well aware of this.

"All right. Let's see who your benefactor is. Got the hologram?"

Father Nuncio reached inside a pocket for his card. He placed it gingerly onto the desk and said, "Image. Confessional." Out of the clear plastic card issued a hologram that filled the room. It was a replica of the confessional box. Within it a program scanned the shape in the darkness that was Pearly.

"What's he wearing, a hood?"

"It looks like it."

"Fuck. What about the voice? Run it through the voice database."

A warbling sound fast-forwarded through Pearly's brief confession. The program searched for a match and, at the same time, generated an intelligent report. The words scrolled across the hologram. *It will take days to search through the database of Manhattan voices alone.*

Gloveless pounded his desk then stood abruptly and cradled his hands on his lower back. He stared out through the glass and observed his recycling facility. "Can't you do a custom scan with that thing? Make the guy's face somehow?"

The priest was secretly glad that the program was failing. He knew the mob wanted to identify the robber so they could use him to destroy Q Bank. "He must have something in his clothing, like we have in the briefcase, blocking, interfering—somehow."

Abruptly the program's warbling halted. Gloveless turned toward the hologram. The card spoke.

In Pearly's voice.

"I've identified the voice. It's my voice. The default voice of the card."

Gloveless's pinprickish eyes widened behind his concave lenses. "His confession is a fucking recording? Smart bastard! God!" He held his hands in prayer and looked up. "God! We need this guy!"

9: Pearly's Blue Room

Pearly looked out through his illuminated exoskull to the vast night sky brilliantly punctuated with starlight. It was not that the light inside him gave him the function of the human eye. He functioned mostly by infrared sensors that illuminated heat sources.

His abode was a penthouse towering high above the dark clouds that end-lessly wrapped Manhattan down below. Only the wealthiest lived in these penthouses, and due to their proximity to sky they were called blue rooms. He had bought it anonymously through an online real estate auction.

He took the card that had played his confession out of a pocket and set it on a table next to the brown paper bag filled with the laundered currency. He could not use his own voice in public. He understood English and Mandarin perfectly, but his mouth and especially his teeth disallowed him to communicate in human languages. He sighed, and a sound like a freight train passing through a tunnel issued out of him.

His teeth, he had recently noticed, were getting a touch dull. He had tried flossing the needles with diamond-grit sandpaper used to polish stone, and it had worked. But he was looking for something more human, especially for getting into the intricate designs carved into his canine teeth.

He was preparing to set out on a journey, one that would take him around the world—or what was left of it—and the amenities of New York City, he knew, could not be expected outside of it. There would be no Chinatown dentists who would clean his teeth in exchange for having their lives spared.

Pearly had all his life but one great wish: to know how he had come to be. He turned his gaze to his large collection of vampire lore, legend, esoterica and even erotica. Word was out on the streets of Chinatown about black market reality, about tapping into parallel realities through it by a process called *jackin' the butterfly*. It was said that the guy who invented it could bring ink to life.

Pearly reconsidered his autobiography. He sat down at his desk where each day he made journal entries fabricating his birth and childhood. He wondered, thinking about Chinatown, if it was possible to write himself into existence. He had discovered more and more, as time went by, that his imagination seemed to have the power to manifest. He lifted a nib and wrote in black india ink: *Oh, sky. You and I are quite alike. Here we are together, undead, and we have no idea why.*

10: Tuxedo Park

The small black helicopter transported Migraine and Jules Barbillon north of Manhattan toward Tuxedo Park.

"How did you get inside Q Bank to see my files?"

Jules's slit pupils narrowed in his golden eyes. "You will find out soon enough."

"I'm just a lead investigator on the ground. Why aren't you taking this offer to someone higher up?"

"We need an ambassador. And much more than that. We need you to actually find out who is robbing the banks. Or act like you have solved it. Our true detective's identity cannot be made known. Ever."

"I'm not a very good actor."

Jules's head snapped on his neck, and he stared at Migraine through his orange-tinted lenses. "We are all great actors in this theater of reality. You just need our script."

"I take that to mean I don't have a choice."

"You're not the only one trying to figure out who the robber is. The Garbage Gang is looking for him also. They want to use him to perform a major and final heist. If Q Bank destabilizes, America, Inc. could go bankrupt."

"That would incite mayhem."

"Exactly."

The helicopter hovered then settled down on a helipad.

Migraine looked out across a dark grassy field to a glass structure blooming with light. "Where are we?"

"Tuxedo Park."

A humanesque robot dressed as a harlequin approached the helicopter, opened the door and motioned for Migraine to follow him. Migraine breathed in the smell of wet grass—something he had never before smelled—and he wondered what it was. All around him the sights, sounds and smells of a rural atmosphere charged his senses. He did not at all like the idea of pretending to solve a crime that someone else was going to, and yet he felt a sense of destiny and excitement like never before. At least not before Q Bank had wiped his memory so that he would not be a security liability.

The harlequin opened the front door and beckoned him inside. Migraine's hard rubber boot soles met a bristled entry mat. The harlequin pointed to his muddy shoes, and Migraine dutifully wiped the mud—which he had also never seen—onto the mat. When he looked up, an elderly bald man with the posture of an exclamation point was standing in front of him. Crinkled eyelids framed his warm brown eyes.

He said, "Welcome. My name is Cosmo Hamilton."

"John Megrim."

"Mr. Megrim, we don't have much time. Not much time at all."

Inside Cosmo's study Migraine took a seat in an overstuffed red leather armchair that was a twin of the one Cosmo sat in. A warm fire burned in the hearth between them. The harlequin offered him a cigar, which he declined.

"So, you're The Broker."

"Yes. Surely you've heard of our services."

"I've heard about them. Why wouldn't Q Bank contact you directly?"

"They do not specifically know that I exist. In the old days people would come to me with their problems. There were just too many crimes to solve in the end. These days we monitor the problems and make ourselves available only to the select few. And we also have a mission."

"Which is?"

"We need to keep our detective alive."

Migraine puzzled over this mission. "I thought you were going to tell me the same thing the guy in the helicopter told me. Some save the world kind of thing."

"Exactly. I'm going to tell you something now that only the very privileged ever get to discover."

"I'm not privileged. I'm a guy who sold his soul to Q Bank."

"I own Q Bank."

Migraine was stunned.

Cosmo stitched his fingers together contemplatively and nodded in affirmation.

"But that isn't what only the privileged get to know. Synthetic currency was developed here by a man named George Black. But that is not all we made here. Here, we made reality."

The study faded away from around them and was replaced by the scintillating, charged space of the Zodiac laboratory.

◆◆◆

In the morning Migraine came to nestled in his sheets, his head cradled by his quantum pillow. The dreamy imagery of Tuxedo Park filled his waking head, and he questioned its validity when he bolted up and saw his front door was not damaged. His doubts washed away when he saw a bullet casing carefully arranged on top of a new black envelope. He scanned the walls of his apartment, somehow knowing he was under full surveillance. He remembered Cosmo telling him they only had seven days to solve the crime, and he cautiously opened the envelope. On the black card was written an address: *113 Ludlow St.*

11: 113 Ludlow St.

Detective Rook Black cut the edge of his egg with a four-pronged fork. It scraped against the cheap porcelain plate. The yolk wiggled, making the pattern of an A surrounded by an O. *Anarchy sign*, he thought, *in my egg?*

Outside the diner named 113 and across the narrow street, huddled under a black umbrella, Migraine observed the doorway. His instructions came back to him in fragments. He still thought it strange that Q Bank would have him tail a detective who they knew could solve the case in seven days. He understood that at best he was some kind of redundancy. *A failsafe*, they had told him. When the door opened and a tall mannequin with a medium muscular build exited, his head bent under a black hat, Migraine knew this was the detective. The hair stood up on the back of his neck, and he thought, *He is going to save the world, and I get to take the credit. Why?*

An inky black rain, the likes of which he had never seen, began to fall.

♦♦♦

Rook slipped into his sedan, his plastic limbs folding with human muscular memory. He had received the lead that morning. It was written inside a black matchbook, an address: *Genesis Avenue*. There were no streets named Genesis Avenue, at least not in Old Manhattan. He thought of mirror writing. "ECHO on. Map," he commanded his windshield computer, "dead ends."

An array of dead end streets populated the screen in his windshield.

Rook turned the ignition.

♦♦♦

Simultaneously the sunjuice vehicle parked in front of Migraine fired up. The driver's window rolled down. There was no one inside. He remembered with a start how they told him things would unfold quickly and unexpectedly. As Q Bank's number-one lead investigator, he was obligated, he had been told, to follow the mannequin man at every turn. The means, they had also told him, would easily be provided. Migraine quickly pressed his palm on the door's reader. Black inky rain followed the outline of his hand. The door unlocked, and he made haste to jump inside. As he tailed the detective's gas-guzzler, a screen in his windshield analyzed data being fed from the sedan. The map of dead ends twinned in the display.

Both cars threaded their way up the Bowery through dense traffic. Just past Houston the detective took a right. Migraine was making the same turn when the sedan halted in the narrow street. Migraine's windows became mirrors, hiding him in reflections. He drove past the detective toward the next intersection. *Damn it! I'm an investigator. Not a spy!*

In the rearview he witnessed Rook double-parking and then getting out of the sedan. Migraine took a hard right, down into a parking garage robot. The robot scanned the sunjuice vehicle and charged it for parking. It's arms rotated toward the car as Migraine leaped out. Back on the sidewalk, fumbling with his umbrella, he spotted the detective scanning an alleyway. A lit digital street sign named it *Extra Place*.

Migraine was about to follow him down it when he realized it had no exit. The detective purposefully strolled to the back wall and stopped a few feet in front of it. The wall was unremarkable, windowless concrete. Inky rain made hatchings in the articulated space between the two men. On the wall it made rivulets that trickled from the pockmarks and scars in the concrete. Rook observed a graffiti tag, of an orange *A* surrounded by an *O*. *Something is dead*, he thought. *Something has come to an end.*

Slowly he pivoted and strode back to his idling sedan.

Migraine, hiding behind a couple of Chinese men lugging a large section of duct work, lost sight of him for a moment, then sprang for the parking garage when he saw the man getting back into his car.

12: Incognito

Pearly stood before a grinning Diamond Geet. He marveled at the man's simple, even teeth. He dared not look past his square cheeks or below the jaw to his neck. He could feel the man's body temperature. Diamond Geet gestured to a small display case, in which the diamond-bristled toothbrush was displayed. The handle was made of ebony. Small diamonds spelled out Pearly's name, modeled after his own elaborate cursive signature. The bristles were silky. Diamond Geet swung a lamp over the case, and a bright reflecting light flashed from the artifact. He was in fact rather proud of his work.

"What do you think?"

Pearly nodded. "I really am not able to thank you enough."

"Please tell your friends!"

"Unfortunately I don't have any."

Diamond Geet was not exactly sure how to handle this comment. He chewed on a lip before smiling broadly again. "I'm sure the toothbrush will change that!"

"Don't try to become one."

Geet's broad grin zipped into a flat line, and he swallowed hard as he witnessed the man's silver skin and long tapering fingers. Geet had assumed the guy was a dada-prosthesist, but now he was not so sure. He tried not to look at the rubber-sheathed hooves.

Pearly opened the lid on the case and removed the toothbrush. It felt cool and solid in his hand. He was anxious to give it a trial. If it was a success, he would be grateful to pack it before he set off to explore the world.

"Tell me, of all the diamond dealers to choose from, why did you choose me?"

"I found the name of your company intriguing." Pearly wrapped the toothbrush in the velvet and stowed it deep inside a pocket. As he made his way to the door, Diamond Geet skittered in front of him and made haste to open the door with a grand gesturing arm.

"Thank you!"

Diamond Geet followed him out to the sidewalk, where Pearly shifted into his sped-up gait and seemed to disappear amongst the pedestrians. Geet looked up at his store sign comprised of lit bare bulbs. It read, *Genesis Gems*.

He noticed that the bulb lighting the dot on the *i* was out.

And from far above him a large drop of blackish ink made gravitational destiny as it aimed for his very precious jeweler's right eye. The drop hit his open eye, and it swirled around the surface of his glossy cornea, making an *A* surrounded by an *O*.

♦♦♦

Pearly stood naked in his bathroom. Shower water pooled at his feet. His pale silvery skin was sinewy and his back was deeply lacerated. The atonement handed out by the priest was never enough to conquer his deep guilt over the murders, and one endless night, when he had imagined a more brutal, punishing form of atonement, he found his imagination overwhelmed with a vision. In this vision a scythe made of something like his teeth, of something glassy and ceramic, manifested. Inside his blue room the scythe manifested fully and became held by a thing invisible. Pinkish red roses ornamented the blade, and as it whirred toward him he turned to run, but it was too late. It was then the scars manifested also, first as razory gashes making an X pattern, then becoming winged things. His wings. The problem with the masochistic atonement by imaginary scythes was, the pain made him more murderous than ever.

He lifted the toothbrush to his left canine and, with a slow rotating motion, he began to polish his teeth.

♦♦♦

Rook Black sat at his desk and massaged the plastic beard bristling on his chin. He studied photos of the *A* surrounded by *O* graffiti. Whoever was doing the tagging in the dead ends was anonymous more than anarchic, he decided. *Anonymous*, he thought, *another word for incognito.*

He stepped back out into the night, the black ink seemingly whispering a chant. *Incognito. Incognito. Incognito.* From inside his sedan he watched as the windshield wipers splashed the ink across the glass, and for a moment they crystallized into porcelain scythes. All around him, in a flash, the pink lights of an advertisement for some Valentine's Day product washed, reflecting roses over the phenomenon.

He turned the key in the ignition, and his gas-guzzler rumbled to life. In a sunjuice vehicle down the street, Migraine's hands tightened on the wheel.

♦♦♦

Jack the Butterfly watered his synthetic roses with a nanographite solution. He felt, in the quantum compression of his lab, the detective coming closer and closer. He heard the knock on the cold steel door before it got there. He watched as blood droplets formed at the tips of the rose thorns and pearls manifested inside the throats of the robust red petals. *Something very, very ancient and very, very evil,* he thought, *is coming home!*

www.ingramcontent.com/pod-product-compliance
Lightning Source LLC
Chambersburg PA
CBHW020614130626
46552CB00007B/3206